Five Little Ducks

illustrated by Penny Ives

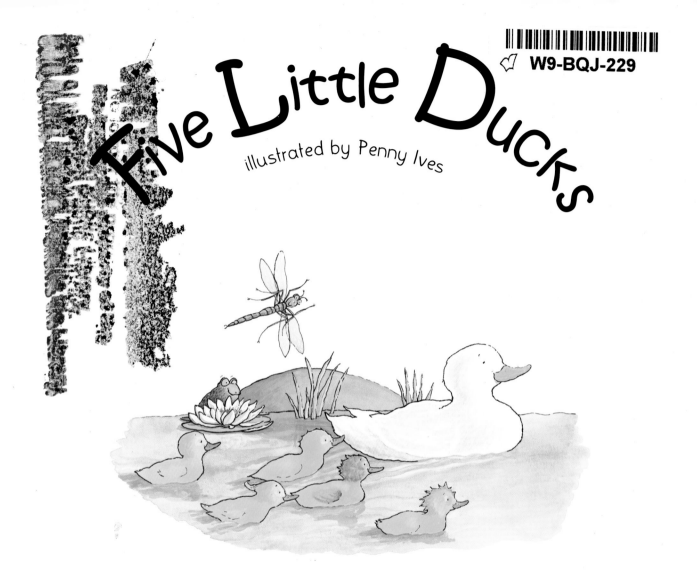

Child's Play (International) Ltd

Ashworth Rd, Bridgemead, Swindon, SN5 7YD UK

Swindon   Auburn ME   Sydney

© 2002 Child's Play (International) Ltd   Printed in Shenzhen, China

ISBN 978-0-85953-447-5   HH0803168X804164475

15 17 19 20 18 16 14

www.childs-play.com

Five little ducks went out one day,

Mother Duck called, "Quack, quack, quack, quack!"

But only four little ducks came back.

Four little ducks went out one day,
Over the hills and far away,

Mother Duck called, "Quack, quack, quack, quack!"
But only three little ducks came back.

Three little ducks went out one day,
Over the hills and far away,

Mother Duck called, "Quack, quack, quack, quack!"
But only two little ducks came back.

Two little ducks went out one day,
Over the hills and far away,

Mother Duck called, "Quack, quack, quack, quack!"
But only one little duck came back.

One little duck went out one day,
Over the hills and far away,

Mother Duck called, "Quack, quack, quack, quack!"
But NO little ducks came back.

No little ducks went out one day,
Over the hills and far away,
Mother Duck called,
"Quack, quack,
quack, quack!"

And five little ducks came wandering back!